Earth

Earth

Written by Francis Davies

Illustrated by Lorenzo Cecchi, Thomas Troyer, Andrea Morandi,
Alessandro Cantucci, and Fabiano Fabbrucci

Gareth Stevens Publishing
A WORLD ALMANAC EDUCATION GROUP COMPANY

Please visit our web site at: www.garethstevens.com
For a free color catalog describing Gareth Stevens Publishing's
list of high-quality books and multimedia programs,
call 1-800-542-2595 or fax your request to (414) 332-3567.

Gareth Stevens Publishing would like to thank Paul Mayer, Geology Collections Manager of the Milwaukee Public Museum, Milwaukee, Wisconsin, for his kind and professional help with the information in this book.

Library of Congress Cataloging-in-Publication Data

Davies, Francis.
    Earth / written by Francis Davies; illustrated by Lorenzo Cecchi ... [et al.].
       p. cm. — (Nature's record-breakers)
    Includes bibliographical references and index.
    ISBN 0-8368-2907-7 (lib. bdg.)
    1. Earth—Juvenile literature. [1. Earth.] I. Cecchi, Lorenzo, ill. II. Title. III. Series.
  QB631.4.D377   2002
  550—dc21   2001020762

This edition first published in 2002 by
Gareth Stevens Publishing
A World Almanac Education Group Company
330 West Olive Street, Suite 100
Milwaukee, Wisconsin 53212 USA

Original edition © 2000 by McRae Books Srl. First published in 2000 as *Planet Earth,* with the series title *Blockbusters!,* by McRae Books Srl., via de' Rustici 5, Florence, Italy. This edition © 2002 by Gareth Stevens, Inc. Additional end matter © 2002 by Gareth Stevens, Inc.

Translated from Italian by Christina Longman
Designer: Marco Nardi
Layout: Ornella Fassio and Adriano Nardi
Gareth Stevens editor: Monica Rausch
Gareth Stevens designer: Scott M. Krall

Printed in the United States of America

1 2 3 4 5 6 7 8 9 06 05 04 03 02

Contents

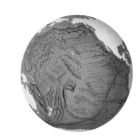

Words that appear in the glossary are printed in **boldface** type
the first time they occur in the text.

Formation and

►Throughout human history, people have had many ideas about Earth's formation and structure. Some believed Earth was a huge dome supported by elephants that were standing on an enormous tortoise. The tortoise rested on a coiled cobra. The cobra was biting its tail in the sky above the highest mountains on Earth.

▼ Most scientists believe Earth was formed about 5 billion years ago. A huge, spinning **nebula**, or cloud of gases and dust in space, began **contracting** from the force of its own **gravity**. Most material in the cloud **condensed** in the center to form the Sun. Some material farther from the center condensed to form the planets.

Sun

nebula

Earth forming

Structure

▲ Earth **orbits**, or travels around, the Sun. This movement — and the tilt of Earth on its axis — creates the different seasons of the year.

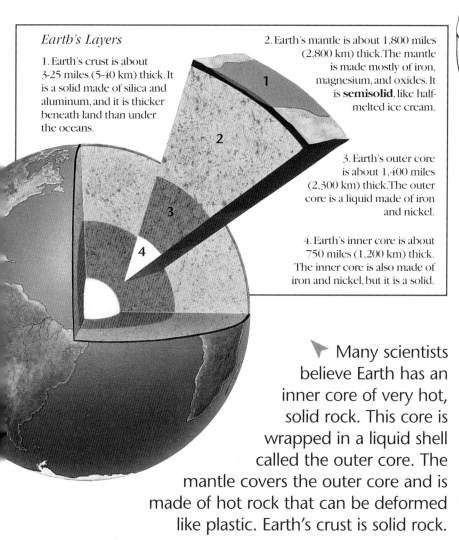

northern spring

northern winter

northern summer

southern autumn

Sun

southern winter

northern autumn

southern spring

southern summer

Earth's Layers

1. Earth's crust is about 3-25 miles (5-40 km) thick. It is a solid made of silica and aluminum, and it is thicker beneath land than under the oceans.

2. Earth's mantle is about 1,800 miles (2,800 km) thick. The mantle is made mostly of iron, magnesium, and oxides. It is **semisolid**, like half-melted ice cream.

3. Earth's outer core is about 1,400 miles (2,300 km) thick. The outer core is a liquid made of iron and nickel.

4. Earth's inner core is about 750 miles (1,200 km) thick. The inner core is also made of iron and nickel, but it is a solid.

▶ Many scientists believe Earth has an inner core of very hot, solid rock. This core is wrapped in a liquid shell called the outer core. The mantle covers the outer core and is made of hot rock that can be deformed like plastic. Earth's crust is solid rock.

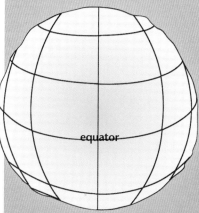
7

Atmosphere

▼ Cirrus, cirrostratus, and cirrocumulus clouds are the highest clouds. These clouds form between 4 and 6 miles (6 and 10 km) above Earth. They are made of tiny ice crystals.

CIRRUS

CIRROSTRATUS

26,000 feet (8,000 m)

◄ Cumulonimbus clouds are the clouds that produce the most thunderstorms. These tall, towering clouds can reach heights of 40,000 feet (12,000 meters). The tops of these clouds are made of ice crystals. Cumulonimbus clouds often form when a body of cold air meets a body of warm air.

CIRROCUMULUS

20,000 feet (6,000 m)

ALTOCUMULUS

13,000 feet (4,000 m)

CUMULONIMBUS

ALTOSTRATUS

▼ Fog is the cloud closest to Earth. Fog forms when moist air reaches a certain temperature and the water in the air condenses to form droplets.

6,500 feet (2,000 m)

STRATOCUMULUS

CUMULUS

STRATUS

NIMBOSTRATUS

FOG

8

➤ Earth's **atmosphere** is the lightest "part" of Earth. Many unique events happen in the atmosphere. Auroras, or waving bands of color in the sky, occur when tiny **particles** from the Sun hit gases in the atmosphere. When rocks or dust from space enter Earth's atmosphere, they burn up, and we see them as fiery meteors.

Fascinating Fact

When Earth was first formed, no plants or animals existed — no oxygen was in the air! Where did Earth's **oxygen** come from? Some scientists believe volcanoes erupted on Earth and released huge amounts of **water vapor**. This vapor condensed into droplets that fell to Earth as rain. The rain eventually filled the oceans. The very first **organisms** developed in the oceans and began producing oxygen. As these organisms grew in number, they produced more and more oxygen.

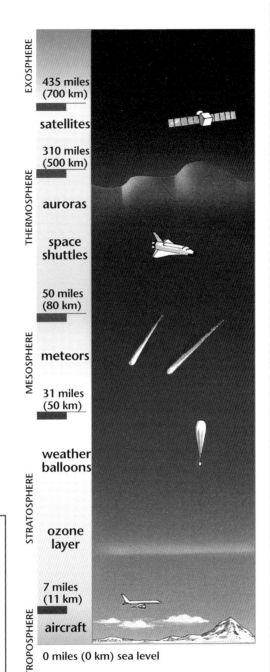

EXOSPHERE

435 miles (700 km)

satellites

310 miles (500 km)

THERMOSPHERE

auroras

space shuttles

50 miles (80 km)

MESOSPHERE

meteors

31 miles (50 km)

weather balloons

STRATOSPHERE

ozone layer

7 miles (11 km)

TROPOSPHERE

aircraft

0 miles (0 km) sea level

Did you know?

Q. WHERE DOES EARTH'S WATER COME FROM?
A. Earth's water was produced billions of years ago when volcanoes erupted and **spewed** enormous amounts of water vapor into the atmosphere.

Q. WHERE DOES RAINWATER COME FROM?
A. Almost all rainwater originally came from Earth's surface. Water in rivers, lakes, and streams; on the leaves of plants; and on the ground **evaporates** in the heat of the Sun and becomes water vapor. This vapor then cools and condenses to form water droplets. The droplets grow in size and eventually fall to Earth as rain.

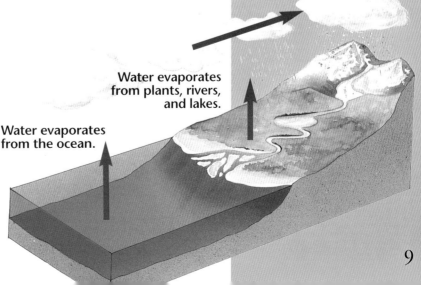

Water evaporates from plants, rivers, and lakes.

Water evaporates from the ocean.

9

Did you know?

Q. WHAT IS A DESERT?

A. A desert is a region that receives less than 10 inches (25 centimeters) of rain, snow, or hail a year. Deserts cover about one-fifth of Earth's surface.

Q. ARE THE SURFACES OF ALL DESERTS MADE OF SAND?

A. No, not all deserts have sandy surfaces. Some desert floors are sheer rock. Others have gravel surfaces, and some deserts even have ice! The most common deserts have a mixture sand, gravel, and rock on their floors.

Q. ARE THE DESERTS SPREADING?

A. Yes, deserts are spreading. Earth's **climate** is changing, and many areas on Earth (shown in red on the map below) are getting drier and drier.

The Sahara Desert is the largest warm desert on Earth. The Sahara is in northern Africa and covers about 3.3 million square miles (8.5 million sq km) — it is almost as big as the United States.

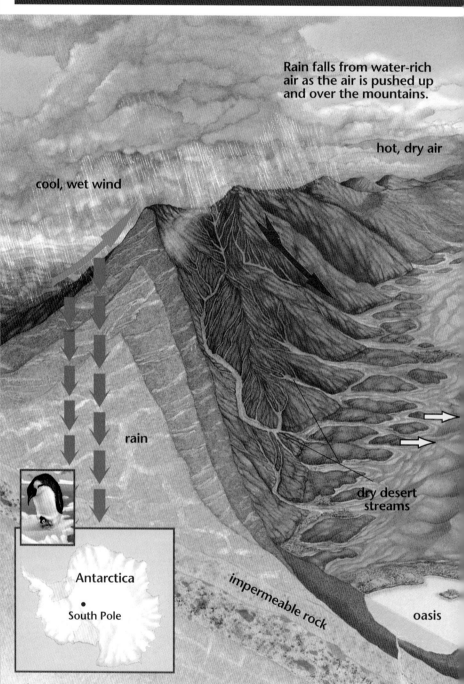

Rain falls from water-rich air as the air is pushed up and over the mountains.

hot, dry air

cool, wet wind

rain

dry desert streams

impermeable rock

oasis

Antarctica

South Pole

Antarctica has the largest cold desert. The continent's polar **plateau** receives only about 2 inches (5 cm) of snow a year. The ice on Antarctica **accumulated** over millions of years as the continent moved toward the South Pole.

Deserts

▼ An oasis is a place where water from below the desert gushes to its surface. To find water in some places in the Sahara Desert, however, wells must be dug over 3,280 feet (1,000 m) deep!

Hot, dry winds blow over the Sahara, drying the desert's surface and wearing down the rocks.

sandy desert

dry winds

chain of dunes

permeable rock

rocky desert

Freshwater

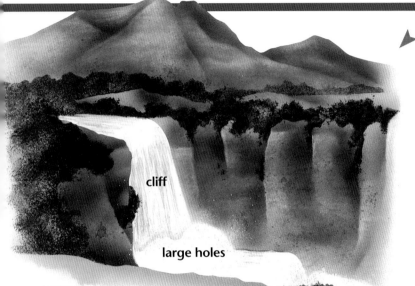

cliff

large holes

▶ A waterfall is one of the most spectacular parts of a river. A waterfall forms when a river plunges over a cliff or a steep, rocky slope. When the water, rocks, and pebbles in the river hit the bottom of the falls, they gradually carve out large holes. Over time, the river also wears down the side of the cliff or slope.

Ten Longest Rivers
(miles/km)

Nile	4,160/6,693
Amazon	4,000/6,436
Yangtze (Chang)	3,964/6,378
Huang (Yellow)	3,395/5,463
Ob-Irtysh	3,362/5,409
Congo	2,900/4,666
Lena	2,734/4,399
Mekong	2,700/4,344
Niger	2,590/4,167
Yenisey	2,543/4,092

Ten Largest Lakes
(square miles/sq km)

Caspian Sea	143,244/371,002
Lake Superior	31,700/82,103
Lake Victoria	26,828/69,484
Lake Huron	23,000/59,570
Lake Michigan	22,300/57,757
Aral Sea	13,000/33,670
Lake Tanganyika	12,700/32,893
Baykal	12,162/31,500
Great Bear Lake	12,096/31,329
Nyasa (Malawi)	11,150/28,879

Mediterranean Sea

Nile Delta

Fayyum oasis

Nile River

Sahara Desert

◀ The Nile River **delta** is one of the most famous deltas in the world. This delta is so wide it can be seen from space! It looks like an enormous green triangle filled with life. Ancient Egyptian peoples flourished in this delta region and created spectacular monuments here.

Along with the great pyramids, the Sphynx is one of the most fascinating ancient Egyptian monuments.

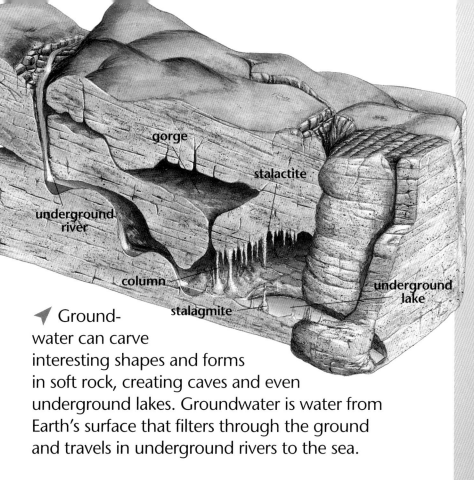

gorge

stalactite

underground river

column

stalagmite

underground lake

◢ Ground-water can carve interesting shapes and forms in soft rock, creating caves and even underground lakes. Groundwater is water from Earth's surface that filters through the ground and travels in underground rivers to the sea.

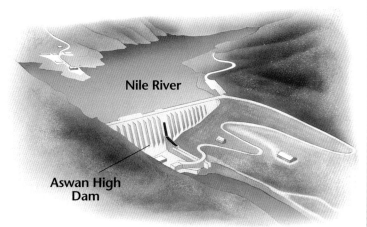

Nile River

Aswan High Dam

◢ The Aswan High Dam on the Nile River in Egypt is one of the most famous dams. The dam produces electricity and provides a regular supply of water for Egypt. The dam, however, has caused some problems. It holds back **silt**, or mud, carried by the river. The silt once fertilized Egyptian fields and formed the river's delta. Now the delta is getting smaller.

Q. HOW DOES A RIVER FORM?

A. A river may form when groundwater rises to the surface as a spring, when a lake overflows, or when ice and snow on high mountain peaks melt. The water from these sources runs downward, and it eventually flows together to form a river. The river runs toward a sea, ocean, or lower body of water. On its way, the river collects rainwater and water from springs, streams, and other rivers.

Q. WHAT IS A RIVER MOUTH?

A. A river mouth is where a river flows into a sea or ocean. River mouths can be different shapes depending on the current of the sea or ocean. If the current is strong, it washes away a river's silt, and the river mouth is a clean, open **estuary**. If the current is weak, the river's silt builds up to form small islands, sand banks, and canals, creating a delta — like the Nile River delta.

Q. WHAT IS A GLACIER?

A. A glacier is a huge river of ice. Just like water in a river, the ice in a glacier flows and "slips" downhill.

Q. HOW DOES A GLACIER FORM?

A. When snow falls in a place where it cannot melt, such as on a high mountain peak, it piles up. As more and more snow falls, the weight of the top layers of snow press down on the lower layers. The older snow on the bottom becomes more and more **compact** and eventually turns into glacial ice.

Q. HOW MUCH FRESHWATER DO GLACIERS HOLD?

A. Earth's glaciers — including the glaciers at the North and South Poles — hold about 77 percent of all the freshwater on the planet.

Q. WHAT IS AN ICE FLOE?

A. An ice floe, or ice pack, is a crust of floating ice that forms when the ocean near the North or South Poles freezes.

Glaciers

▲ The largest iceberg ever recorded was 207 miles (333 km) long and 62 miles (100 km) wide. This huge slab of ice was spotted off of Antarctica in 1956 by the USS *Glacier*. Only about 14 percent of an iceberg can be seen above the water. Icebergs form in polar oceans. Sea waters here freeze in winter, and the ice cracks and breaks apart when it thaws in spring.

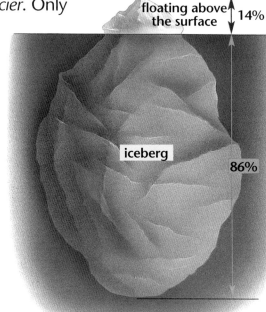

floating above the surface 14%

iceberg

86%

arctic glaciers during the last ice age (A) and today (B)

A

B

◤ The coldest climate on Earth existed during the ice ages, the times in Earth's history when huge areas of land were covered by glaciers. Much of Earth's water was frozen in the glaciers and did not reach the oceans. The water levels in oceans fell, and lands once separated by water were joined.

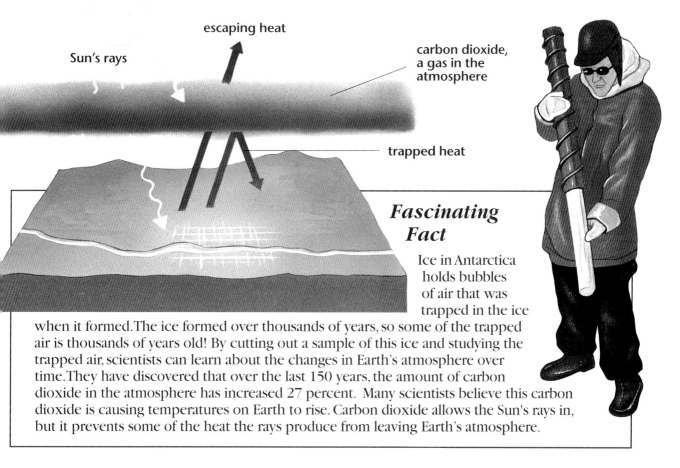

escaping heat

Sun's rays

carbon dioxide, a gas in the atmosphere

trapped heat

Fascinating Fact

Ice in Antarctica holds bubbles of air that was trapped in the ice when it formed. The ice formed over thousands of years, so some of the trapped air is thousands of years old! By cutting out a sample of this ice and studying the trapped air, scientists can learn about the changes in Earth's atmosphere over time. They have discovered that over the last 150 years, the amount of carbon dioxide in the atmosphere has increased 27 percent. Many scientists believe this carbon dioxide is causing temperatures on Earth to rise. Carbon dioxide allows the Sun's rays in, but it prevents some of the heat the rays produce from leaving Earth's atmosphere.

The Huggard Glacier in Alaska is the largest glacier outside the polar areas. This glacier is 93 miles (150 km) long! The length of Earth's glaciers is constantly changing, however. As Earth's average temperature rises and Earth warms, the glaciers are melting.

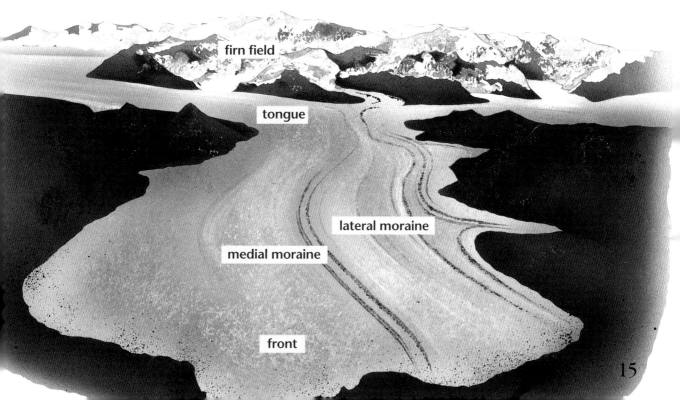

firn field

tongue

lateral moraine

medial moraine

front

Did you know?

Q. How do mountains form?

A. Earth's crust is constantly moving, or shifting. As the crust shifts, sections of the crust are sometimes pushed upward, forming mountains. When two pieces of the crust carrying continents collide, for example, the crust crumples like the body of a car in a car crash, and rocks in the crust are pushed upward.

Q. How can we tell how old a mountain is?

A. We can tell how old a mountain is by looking at its shape and size. The youngest mountains — mountains that are "only" tens of millions of years old — have pointed, rough shapes with jagged peaks, deep canyons, and sharp cliffs. Young mountains are usually very high, too. Old mountains — mountains a billion or so years old — are rounded. Wind, water, ice, and the heat of the Sun have had more time to **erode**, or wear down, the edges of these mountains, and now they look almost like large hills.

The Himalayas form the highest mountain chain on Earth. This chain has thirty towering peaks over 25,000 feet (7,620 m) high — and these mountains are still growing!

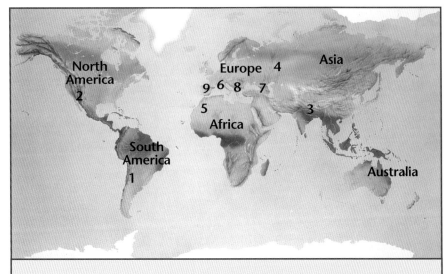

The Longest Mountain Chains in the World and Their Highest Peaks
(length in miles/km)   (height in feet/m)

		length in miles/km		height in feet/m
1	Andes	4,500/7,240	Aconcagua	22,834/6,960
2	Rocky Mountains	3,000/4,830	Elbert	14,433/4,399
3	Himalayas	1,550/2,490	Everest	29,035/8,850
4	Urals	1,500/2,410	Narodnaya	6,217/1,895
5	Atlas Mountains	1,500/2,410	Jebel Toubkal	13,665/4,165
6	Alps	750/1,210	Mont Blanc	15,771/4,807
7	Caucasus Mountains	750/1,210	Elbrus	18,510/5,642
8	Balkans	330/530	Botev	7,795/2,376
9	Pyrenees	270/430	Pico de Aneto	11,168/3,404

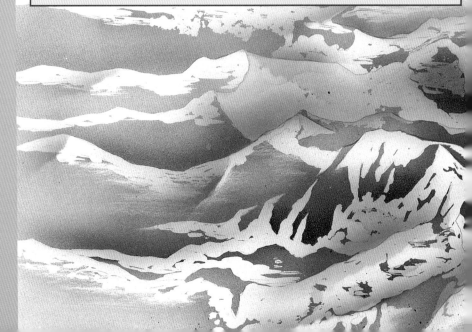

Mountains

◀ The edges of continents have the most mountain chains. Earth's few inland mountain chains mark the edges of ancient continents that were pushed together over time and are now joined.

Fascinating Fact

Some rocks contain **fossils**. If organisms die and are quickly covered by mud, they sometimes **decompose** very slowly, and each tiny part of their bodies is replaced by a rock particle. The mud around the organisms also hardens into rock, encasing the animals. Today the fossils of these animals appear in the rocks where they were trapped. These fossils can be millions of years old.

▼ Antarctica is the highest continent on Earth, with an average elevation of 7,500 feet (2,300 m). This continent of long plateaus and tall peaks lies under a thick blanket of ice.

▼ Europe is the lowest continent on Earth, with an average elevation of just 1,100 feet (340 m) above sea level. In fact, three-fifths of Europe's land is less than 600 feet (180 m) in elevation!

Did you know?

Q. WHY ARE OCEANS AND SEAS SALTY?

A. Oceans and seas are formed by water carried to them by rivers. The water in rivers picks up some salt from the ground as it travels. As more and more water pours into seas and oceans, this salt accumulates. Also, when water evaporates from seas and oceans, the salt in the evaporating water is left behind. Over thousands of years, seas and oceans gradually become more and more salty.

Q. WHY DO COLD SEAS HAVE MORE FISH?

A. The cold water in cold seas can hold more oxygen than warm water. This oxygen helps algae, a plantlike food many sea animals eat, grow and reproduce more easily. Algae attract animals — such as fish. Cold seas also have more fish because deep ocean currents, which contain lots of nutrients for fish, rise in cold seas.

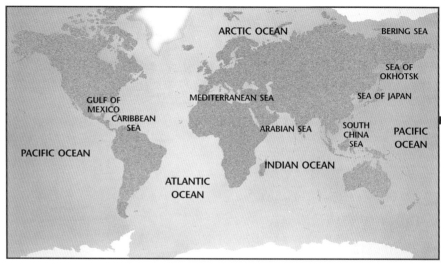

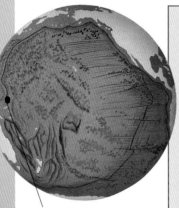

The *Trieste* dove a record 35,802 feet (10,912 m) into the trench.

Ten Largest Oceans and Seas and Their Deepest Points		
	(million square miles/million sq km)	(depth in feet/m)
Pacific Ocean	64/166	36,203/11,034
Atlantic Ocean	33/87	28,232/8,605
Indian Ocean	28/73	23,376/7,125
Arctic Ocean	5.1/13	17,881/5,450
South China Sea	1.1/2.8	18,238/5,559
Caribbean Sea	.97/2.5	24,720/7,535
Mediterranean Sea	.97/2.5	16,896/5,150
Bering Sea	.87/2.3	13,422/4,091
Sea of Okhotsk	.54/1.4	11,155/3,400
Sea of Japan	.39/1.0	13,862/4,225

▶ The Mariana **Trench** in the Pacific Ocean is the lowest point on Earth's surface. In this trench, the ocean is 6.8 miles (11 km) deep.

Mid-Atlantic Ridge on the floor of the Atlantic Ocean

▶ The oceanic ridges, or mountain chains on the ocean floor, are the longest chains of volcanoes. Gases escape from these volcanoes and immediately dissolve in ocean waters. Hot, **molten** rock, or lava, from the volcanoes hardens on contact with the water.

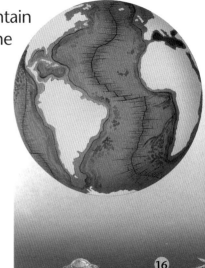

Saltwater

Waves are the most **visible** movements in oceans. When the wind blows, it moves water on the surface of oceans and causes the water to travel in a circle. As an ocean becomes shallower, the moving water cannot complete an entire circle. Its path becomes more oval in shape, until finally the water can not "roll," and it "breaks."

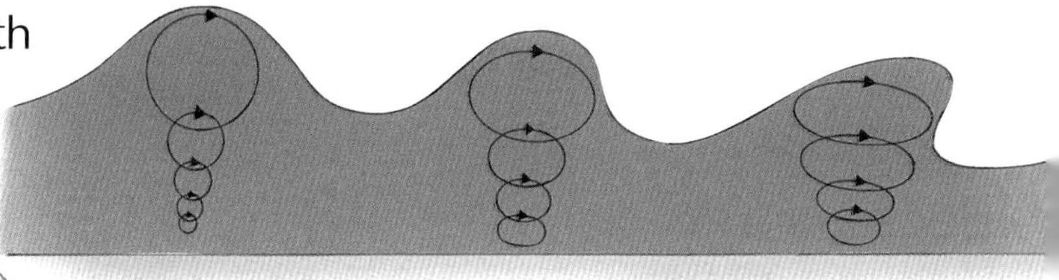

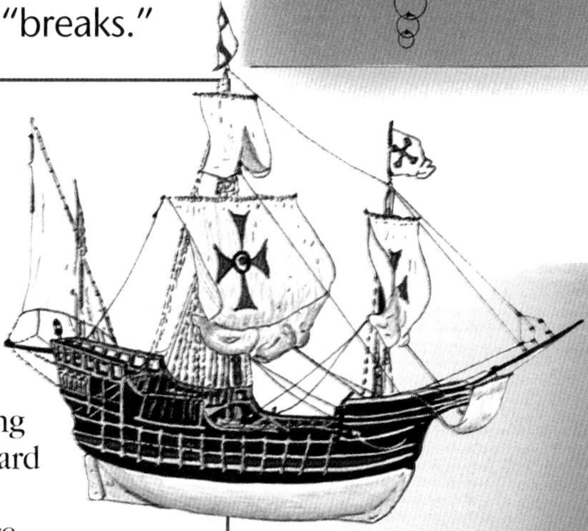

Fascinating Fact

Christopher Columbus landed in the Americas with the help of ocean currents and the trade winds, strong winds that blow toward the southwest in the Northern Hemisphere. The journey home to Europe — sailing against the winds — was more difficult!

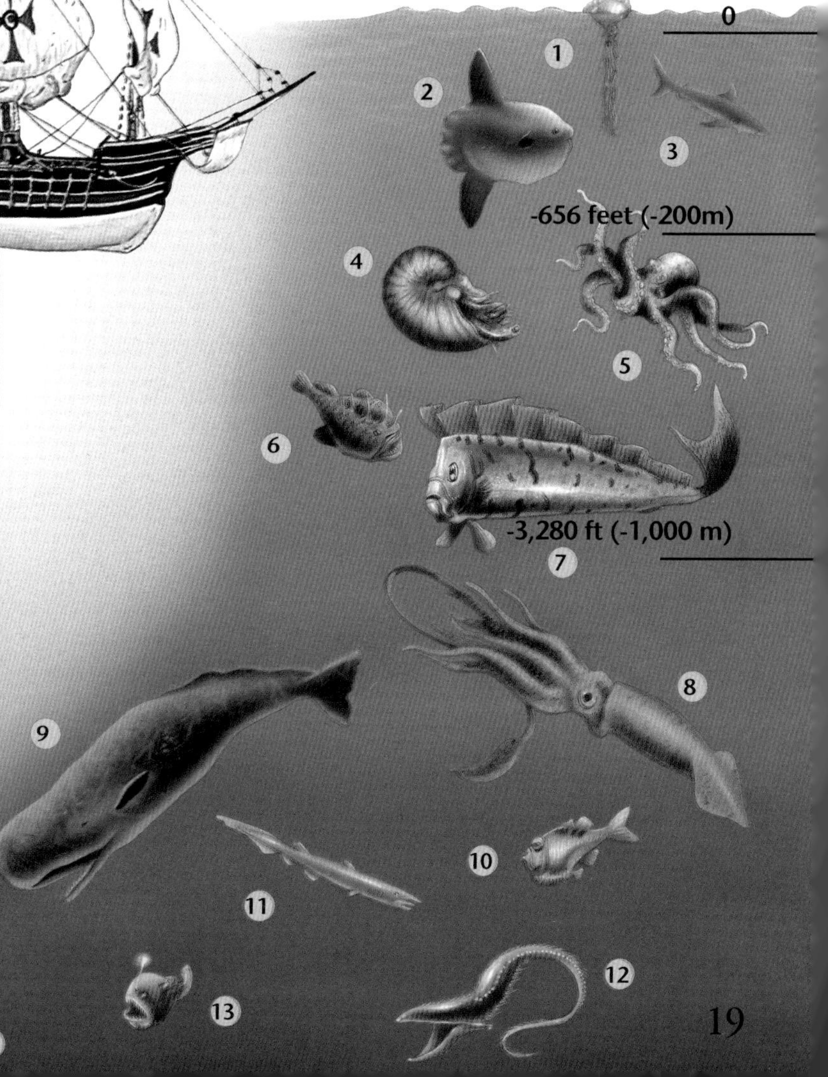

1	Portuguese man of war	10	hatchetfish
2	sunfish	11	goblin shark
3	big nose shark	12	pelican fish
4	nautilus	13	larval fish
5	octopus	14	giant anglerfish
6	anglerfish	15	tripod fish
7	ribbon fish	16	angular rough shark
8	giant squid	17	deep sea jellyfish
9	sperm whale		

0

-656 feet (-200m)

-3,280 ft (-1,000 m)

Rocks, Minerals, and Precious Stones

The crown jewels of the British Empire are some of the world's most precious stones. St. Edward's Crown (left) is set with 444 precious stones and weighs almost 5 pounds (2 kilograms). Another British crown, the Imperial State Crown, is decorated with over 3,000 gems, including the Black Prince's Ruby, a red stone that is the size of an egg.

magnetite

Fascinating Fact

Magnetite, a black, slightly shiny iron mineral, may look like an ordinary rock, but it has a unique property — it attracts other types of iron! If a tiny piece of magnetite is placed near a compass, the compass needle will move from its normal position — pointing to the North Pole — and point toward the magnetite.

Iceland spar, a form of pure calcite, can make humans see double! When light travels through this mineral, it is split into two rays, so, when you look through Iceland spar, one object will appear as two objects.

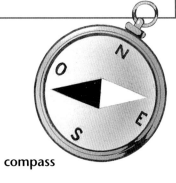
compass

➤ Amber is a hard mineral that once was gooey. Amber is **fossilized** resin, a sticky **substance** that oozes from trees. Amber can contain tiny insects. Millions of years ago, these insects were trapped in the resin and fossilized.

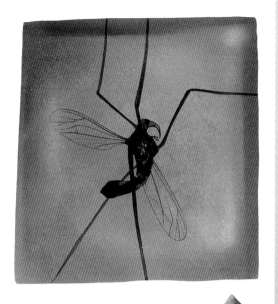

◀ Diamonds are the hardest minerals. To measure how hard a mineral is, scientists compare it to a mineral on Mohs Scale (right). For example, if a mineral scratches talc but not rock salt, it is harder than talc but softer than rock salt.

DIAMOND 10

CORUNDUM 9

TOPAZ 8

QUARTZ 7

ORTHOCLASE FELDSPAR 6

APATITE 5

FLUOROSPAR 4

CALCITE 3

ROCK SALT 2

TALC 1

Mohs Scale

➤ Turquoise is one of the first stones humans used for decoration. The Mayan people of Central America used this blue-green mineral to decorate temples. Precious stones and gems are just polished minerals humans find beautiful.

Did you know?

Q. WHAT ARE MINERALS?
A. Minerals are not living substances. They are formed naturally and are not made by humans. Each mineral is made of a single substance that cannot be broken down into other, simpler substances. The **atoms** of minerals are arranged in set patterns to form solid units called crystals.

Q. WHAT ARE ROCKS?
A. Rocks are mixtures of different minerals. Three main types of rock exist: igneous, sedimentary, and metamorphic. Igneous rocks are hardened lava. Sedimentary rocks are formed when loose material, or sediment, from older rocks, plants, and animals hardens over time. Metamorphic rocks are rocks that were changed and formed by heat or pressure.

Q. WHAT IS A CARAT?
A. A carat is a unit of weight measurement used for precious stones. One carat is equal to .007 ounces (.2 grams).

Earthquakes

Q. WHAT IS AN EARTHQUAKE?

A. An earthquake is the shaking of ground caused by a movement of Earth's crust.

Q. WHAT ARE SEISMIC WAVES?

A. Seismic waves are the movements in rocks caused by an earthquake. This movement is like the ripples produced by a stone dropped in a puddle of water — the earthquake sets off a series of waves that quickly spread out and pass through the rocks on Earth.

Q. WHAT IS A SEISMOGRAPH?

A. A seismograph is a machine that measures the strength and direction of seismic waves.

Q. WHAT IS A VOLCANO?

A. A volcano is a vent or crack in Earth's crust through which gases, vapor, hot water, and lava, or molten rock, escape.

◀ In about A.D. 132, Chinese astronomer Chang Heng built the first instrument for finding the direction of an earthquake. As the ground shook, a ball in a dragon's mouth at the top of the instrument fell onto a frog lying in the same direction as the source of the seismic waves.

Earthquakes can cause severe damage to cities.

This bronze model of a sheep's liver was used by the Etruscans to predict the future.

Fascinating Fact

The ancient Etruscans, a people living in Italy around 700 B.C., believed they could predict future events — including earthquakes — by looking at animal organs. Other people tried to predict quakes by watching the behavior of animals because they believed animals could "sense" when an earthquake was about to hit. Today, scientists have found no proof that these methods really work, and they are still looking for a reliable way to predict earthquakes and movements in Earth's crust.

and Volcanoes

A

B

C

D

➤ The eruption of Mount Saint Helens, a composite volcano, was one of the most powerful volcanic events ever recorded in North America. The explosion blasted away the top of the mountain's peak. Composite volcanoes (A) are tall volcanoes that spew fluid and rocky lava.

➤ Parícutin, a cinder cone volcano in Mexico, started as a hole in a corn field and grew to over 328 feet (100 m) in five days! In two years, it reached its final height of 1,345 feet (410 m). Cinder cone volcanoes (B) are usually small and spew loose, rocky lava.

➤ Mauna Loa, a shield volcano on the island of Hawaii, is Earth's largest active volcano. Shield volcanoes (C) have broad, domed tops that look like a warrior's shield. Mauna Loa's lava flow covers almost 2,000 square miles (5,180 sq km).

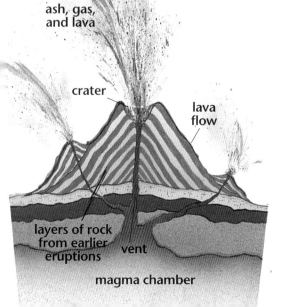

ash, gas, and lava

crater

lava flow

layers of rock from earlier eruptions

vent

magma chamber

◀ The greatest lava eruption in recorded history happened at Laki fissure in Iceland. A fissure is a huge crack in Earth's crust. Fissure vents (D) are relatively flat volcanoes. Laki erupted from June 1783 to February 1784 and spewed 2.95 cubic miles (12.3 cubic km) of lava.

23

The Moving Earth

▲ The plate tectonics theory is the most accepted explanation for the pattern of earthquakes and volcanoes on Earth. According to this theory, Earth's crust is made up of plates that shift and move, bumping into one another. Earthquakes and volcanoes occur most often in the places where these plates meet.

North American Plate

Eurasian Plate

Arabic plate

Caribbean Plate

African Plate

Philippine Plate

Pacific Plate

Cocos Plate

Pacific Plate

Indian Plate

Nazca Plate

South American Plate

Antarctic Plate

▲ Antarctica is the one continent that will probably be in the same position 100,000 years from now.

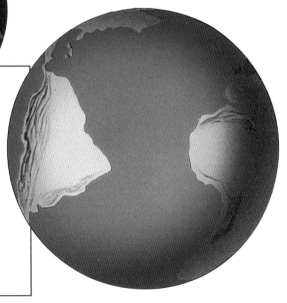

Fascinating Fact

In the early 1900s, Alfred Wegener discovered that the continents fit together like puzzle pieces. The eastern edge of South America, for example, fit perfectly with the western coast of Africa. He believed all the continents on Earth once formed one large continent, called Pangaea. Over time, the continents moved apart. His idea was called continental drift. Later, the plate tectonics theory helped explain how the continents moved.

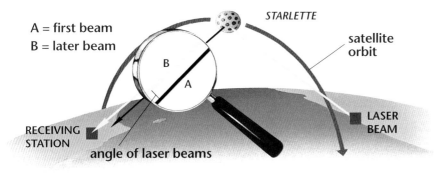

A = first beam
B = later beam

STARLETTE

satellite orbit

LASER BEAM

RECEIVING STATION

angle of laser beams

◀ *Starlette*, a satellite launched in 1975, is one of the few machines used to measure how fast Earth's crust is shifting. *Starlette* is a sphere, or ball, covered with 60 small mirrors. Laser beams shot from one continent hit one of the mirrors and bounce back to another continent. Scientists study the position of the satellite and the changing angles of the laser beams to see how fast the two continents are moving.

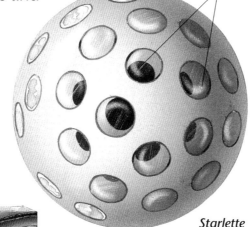

mirrors

Starlette

two plates move apart

volcano

upward flow of molten rock

◀ The most spectacular cracks in Earth's crust are on the ocean floors. Scientists believe two plates are moving away from each other along some of these cracks, or fissures. Molten rock from the mantle rises to Earth's surface here.

New Oceans and
New Continents

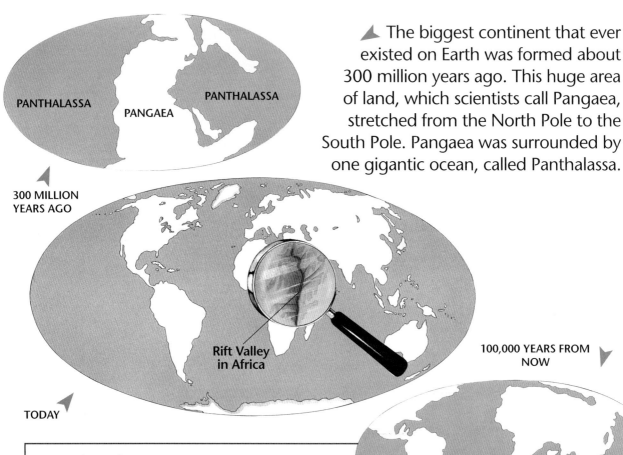

▲ The biggest continent that ever existed on Earth was formed about 300 million years ago. This huge area of land, which scientists call Pangaea, stretched from the North Pole to the South Pole. Pangaea was surrounded by one gigantic ocean, called Panthalassa.

PANTHALASSA

PANTHALASSA

PANGAEA

300 MILLION YEARS AGO

Rift Valley in Africa

100,000 YEARS FROM NOW

TODAY

Fascinating Facts

• The world's newest ocean is forming in the Rift Valley, a long trench in the heart of Africa. The valley runs from the Red Sea in northern Africa to the coast of the Indian Ocean in southern Africa. As the sides of the valley continue to move away from each other, sea water will eventually flow into the valley from the Red Sea and the Indian Ocean and fill it.

• Some scientists are predicting how Earth's crust will move over the next 100,000 years. They believe Africa, Europe, and Asia will push together to form a single continent. Eastern Africa will split away from the rest of Africa, while Australia, Indonesia, and the Philippines will link to South Asia. The Americas will continue to move westward, and California will break away from North America.

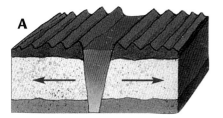

A

B

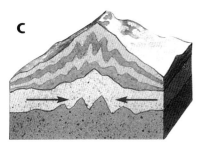

C

D

▶ Earth's plates move in two main ways: they can move away from one another (A), as they do along the oceanic ridges, or they can push together and collide. When they push against one another, one plate may slip over the other (B). If the plates carry continents, the plates may push rocks on the edges of these continents up to the surface (C). The rocks form huge mountain chains. When the Indian and Asian plates collided, for example, the Himalayas were born. Two plates can also slide past one another in jerks (D), and each jerk results in a new earthquake.

▶ The Grand Canyon in Arizona was formed over billions of years. The water in the Colorado River wore a path through rocks and carved out the canyon. In some places, the canyon is 6,234 feet (1,900 m) deep!

Colorado River

Did you
know?

Q. HOW DO WE KNOW THAT THE CONTINENTS WERE STILL JOINED TOGETHER **200** MILLION YEARS AGO?

A. Scientists study where fossils are located, how fast the oceanic ridges and other mountain ranges are growing, and how the Earth's crust is shifting today to discover what Earth may have looked like 200 million years ago.

Q. HOW CAN CONTINENTS "SINK" INTO THE MANTLE?

A. Continents can sink into the mantle because the mantle is not completely solid — it acts somewhat like a liquid, like half-melted ice cream. When two continents collide, sometimes the lighter continent is pushed up while the heavier continent is pushed down into the mantle, like a spoon pushed down into soft ice cream.

Did you know?

Q. HOW DID LIFE ON EARTH BEGIN?

A. Scientists believe life began in the oceans, when chemical molecules **evolved**, or changed over time, to form the first **single-celled** organisms. These organisms further evolved to become **multicelled** organisms. Over millions of years, the multicelled organisms evolved to form the living beings on Earth today.

Q. IS THERE LIFE ON OTHER PLANETS?

A. No one has a definite answer to this question, but scientists are studying information gathered by spacecraft sent to Mars and Europa, Jupiter's moon, to determine whether life ever existed there.

Insects are the group of animals that have the most **species**, with more than 751,000 different species. There are "only" 5,000 species of mammals — and one of them is the human being.

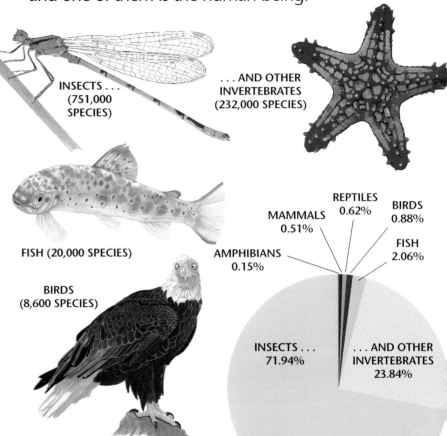

INSECTS . . . (751,000 SPECIES)

. . . AND OTHER INVERTEBRATES (232,000 SPECIES)

FISH (20,000 SPECIES)

BIRDS (8,600 SPECIES)

MAMMALS 0.51%

AMPHIBIANS 0.15%

REPTILES 0.62%

BIRDS 0.88%

FISH 2.06%

INSECTS . . . 71.94%

. . . AND OTHER INVERTEBRATES 23.84%

Fascinating Fact

Some scientists believe the first forms of life on Earth were probably simple bacteria that could survive hot temperatures. Bacteria similar to these first life forms still live in hot waters near geysers and oceanic ridges.

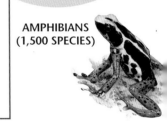

AMPHIBIANS (1,500 SPECIES)

REPTILES (6,000 SPECIES)

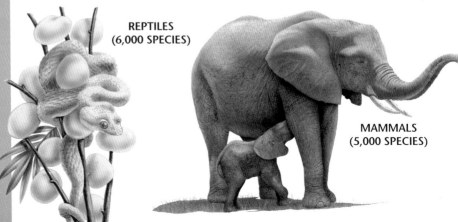

MAMMALS (5,000 SPECIES)

The Living Planet

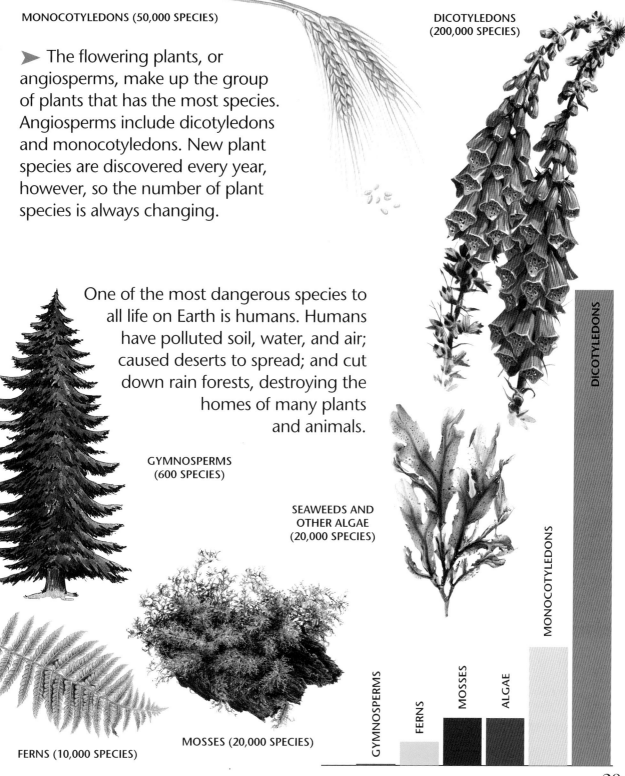

MONOCOTYLEDONS (50,000 SPECIES)

➤ The flowering plants, or angiosperms, make up the group of plants that has the most species. Angiosperms include dicotyledons and monocotyledons. New plant species are discovered every year, however, so the number of plant species is always changing.

DICOTYLEDONS
(200,000 SPECIES)

One of the most dangerous species to all life on Earth is humans. Humans have polluted soil, water, and air; caused deserts to spread; and cut down rain forests, destroying the homes of many plants and animals.

GYMNOSPERMS
(600 SPECIES)

SEAWEEDS AND
OTHER ALGAE
(20,000 SPECIES)

FERNS (10,000 SPECIES)

MOSSES (20,000 SPECIES)

GYMNOSPERMS
FERNS
MOSSES
ALGAE
MONOCOTYLEDONS
DICOTYLEDONS

Glossary

accumulated: built up, collected, or gathered over a period of time.

atmosphere: all the gases that surround Earth.

atom: the smallest unit of a chemical that can exist on its own.

climate: the average weather conditions over a period of time. A desert, for example, receives very little rain and therefore has a dry climate.

compact: closely packed together.

condensed: became more closely or tightly packed together.

contracting: moving closer or squeezing together to become smaller.

decompose: break down slowly; rot.

delta: a triangular area of land formed where a river meets an ocean or sea. The land is made of silt deposited by the river.

equator: an imaginary line that circles Earth exactly halfway between the North Pole and the South Pole.

erode: wear down over time.

estuary: an area where a river meets a sea or ocean, and the current of the sea or ocean washes away silt carried by the river.

evaporates: changes into a vapor or gas.

evolved: developed or changed shape gradually over a long period of time.

fossilized: decomposed slowly over time to become a fossil.

fossils: traces or remains of animals or plants from an earlier period of time that are often found in rock.

gravity: the force that causes objects like the Sun and its planets to be attracted to one another.

molten: melted.

multicelled: made up of more than one cell. A cell is the smallest part of an organism.

nebula: a cloud of gases and dust in space.

orbits: (v) travels around an object.

organisms: living things.

oxygen: a gas found in Earth's atmosphere. All living things need oxygen to survive.

particles: very tiny pieces of a substance.

plateau: a large area of high, flat land.

semisolid: acting somewhat like a solid, being firm and keeping a certain shape, and somewhat like a liquid, flowing and reshaping easily. Half-melted ice cream is a semisolid.

silt: tiny pieces of sand and dirt carried by water that eventually settle on the bottoms of rivers, lakes, or oceans.

single-celled: made up of only one cell, the smallest unit of an organism.

species: animals or plants that are closely related. Members of the same species can breed together.

spewed: gushed or shot out from; erupted.

substance: the basic material out of which something is made.

trench: a deep, long, narrow ditch or valley.

visible: able to be seen.

water vapor: tiny drops of water floating in air; steam.

More Books to Read

The Blue and Green Ark: An Alphabet for Planet Earth. Brian Patten (Scholastic Trade)

Earth Child 2000: Earth Science for Young Children: Games, Stories, Activities, and Experiments. Kathryn Sheehan and Mary Waldner (Council Oak Distribution)

I Wonder Why the Wind Blows and Other Questions about Our Planet. I Wonder Why (series). Anita Ganeri (Kingfisher Books)

Icebergs, Ice Caps, and Glaciers. Rookie Read-About (series). Allan Fowler (Children's Press)

The Living Earth. Eleonore Schmid (North South Books)

The Nature and Science of Rocks. Exploring the Science of Nature (series). Jane Burton and Kim Taylor (Gareth Stevens)

Planet Earth: Inside Out. Gail Gibbons (Mulberry Books)

Rocks and Minerals. Eyewitness Explorers (series). Steve Parker (DK Publishing)

The Science of Soil. Living Science (series). Jonathan Bocknek (Gareth Stevens)

Videos

Earth Science for Children (series). (Schlessinger)

Rocks and Minerals. Science in Action (series). (Vision Quest Video)

Water Cycle. (Library Video)

Weather and Climate Fundamentals. (SVE and Churchill Media)

Web Sites

All About Glaciers
nsidc.org/glaciers/information.html

Earth Floor: Plate Tectonics
www.cotf.edu/ete/modules/msese/earthsysflr/plates1.html

Rock Hound
www.fi.edu/fellows/payton/rocks/index2.html

A Wonderful World of Minerals
library.thinkquest.org/J002744/adlm.html

Some web sites stay current longer than others. For further web sites, use a search engine, such as www.yahooligans.com, to locate the following keywords: *deserts, Earth, earthquakes, fossils, geology, glaciers, ice, mountains, plate tectonics, volcanoes,* and *water cycle.*

Index